# Mama Bear

# Mama Bear

### CHYNG FENG SUN

*Illustrated by* LOLLY ROBINSON

Houghton Mifflin Company    Boston  1994

給那些努力了而仍得不到的

*To those who try but haven't succeeded — C.F.S.*

*To my family — L.R.*

We want to thank Krystal Yung and her mother, Helen, and the real Mrs. Wong—Mary SooHoo—for being the models for this book.

Text copyright © 1994 by Chyng Feng Sun
Illustrations copyright © 1994 by Lolly Robinson

*Library of Congress Cataloging-in-Publication Data*

Sun, Chyng Feng.
  Mama bear / Chyng Feng Sun ; illustrated by Lolly Robinson.
    p.   cm.
  Summary: When Mei-Mei fails in her attempt to earn money through a cookie sale for the expensive toy bear she wants for Christmas, her mother helps her see a special gift she has had all along.
    ISBN 0-395-63412-1
  [1. Chinese Americans—Fiction.   2. Moneymaking projects—Fiction.
3. Restaurants—Fiction.   4. Christmas—Fiction.]      I. Robinson, Lolly, ill.   II. Title.
PZ7.S9565Mam   1994                92-9111
[E]—dc20                    CIP
                           AC

Printed in the United States of America
BP   10   9   8   7   6   5   4   3   2   1

"Mama, look!" said Mei-Mei.

"It's cute, isn't it? Would you like to go in and take a good look?" Mother asked.

"Oh, yes."

Mother took Mei-Mei's hand and entered the store. Mei-Mei's arms circled the bear in a big hug. "It's the softest, warmest bear in the whole world," said Mei-Mei. Mother glanced at the price tag but didn't say anything.

On the way home, Mei-Mei could think of nothing but the bear. "Mama, if I could hold it when I sleep, I wouldn't feel cold." Then she had a better idea. "Mama, we could both hold it. The three of us would feel very, very warm."

Her mother sighed. "Mei-Mei, I know you want the bear for Christmas, but I must tell you something. The bear is just too expensive. I won't get a raise at Chef Wong's until Chinese New Year in February. And you know our heater has to be fixed before the weather gets really cold. I'm afraid there won't be anything left for—"

"But, Mama," Mei-Mei said, and pulled herself closer to her mother, "if we had the bear, we wouldn't need the heater. We could hug the bear. It would keep us warm."

Her mother smiled. "Mei-Mei, how can I hold the bear while I am washing dishes?" She was silent for a minute. "Last winter when I saw you wearing your coat inside and two layers of socks to bed, I felt—I felt so . . ."

Mei-Mei hugged her mother. "Mama, it's OK. We'll fix the heater."

At home, Mei-Mei hunted through all the cabinets and finally found what she wanted, a glass vase. "I will save money for our bear, our Christmas present," Mei-Mei announced. Mother opened her purse and threw in a quarter, two dimes, and four pennies. When the coins clinked, Mei-Mei clapped her hands. "They sound so beautiful."

Every Tuesday and Thursday, Mother got off work early, so Mei-Mei went to Chef Wong's after school instead of Aunt Lin's house. Then Mei-Mei and Mother walked home together. On her way to the restaurant, Mei-Mei would stop at the store window and check to see if her bear was still there.

One Tuesday the restaurant was unusually busy. Customers lined up at the door and the waitresses hurried by carrying plates piled high with food. Sitting by the counter, Mei-Mei noticed that a little pool of soy sauce was left on a table close to her. She picked up a handful of napkins and wiped the table clean.

Soon it was time for Mei-Mei and her mother to go home. Mrs. Wong, the owner, smiled at Mei-Mei and said, "Thank you for helping out, you good little worker." Then she gave Mei-Mei an almond cookie.

The minute they stepped outside, Mei-Mei tore the wrapping paper off the cookie. She was going to take a bite when she stopped and raised the cookie to her mother's mouth. "Mama, want a bite?"

"No, thank you," said Mother. "It's all yours."

Mei-Mei savored the cookie in tiny bites.

The next week on her way to Chef Wong's, Mei-Mei found a maple leaf twig. At the restaurant, she put it in an empty soy sauce jar on a table beside the window.

"How beautiful!" a woman's voice surprised Mei-Mei as she was admiring what she had done. "What a nice idea!"

That evening, Mrs. Wong gave her two almond cookies, and said, "You are quite an artist!" After that, when Mei-Mei went to the restaurant, Mrs. Wong would find small jobs for her and give her almond cookies. Mei-Mei ate only one cookie a day and saved the extra ones for the days she didn't go to the restaurant. She liked to eat one while her mother read her a story. Afterward, Mother would throw a few coins in the vase, and they both listened to the clinks.

One day when Mei-Mei was working, a customer came in and ordered some dishes to go. "How much are the almond cookies?" he asked.

"One dollar each," said Mrs. Wong.

Mei-Mei almost fell off her stool. One dollar each? She must have eaten at least ten dollars' worth of cookies in the last month. Mei-Mei thought of the bear waiting for her all that time and she wanted to cry.

From that day on, Mei-Mei stopped eating the precious cookies. She saved them without knowing what to do with them. She hoped they would somehow turn into money.

She finally got an idea.

"Could I have a sale in your restaurant?" Mei-Mei asked Mrs. Wong. She explained about the bear for her and her mother.

"What do you want to sell?" asked Mrs. Wong.

"Almond cookies," Mei-Mei said in a serious voice.

"What? My cookies? The cookies I gave you?" Mrs. Wong looked very surprised.

Mei-Mei rushed to explain. "I love your almond cookies. But when I found out how much they cost, I stopped eating them and now I have ten. I want to sell them for money to buy my bear."

"I see." Mrs. Wong asked, "How much do you want to sell them for?"

Mei-Mei thought for a moment. "One dollar and fifty cents."

"Mei-Mei," Mrs. Wong said, shaking her head, "if your cookies cost more than mine, who will buy yours?"

Mei-Mei reconsidered. "One dollar, just like yours?"

Mrs. Wong shook her head again.

"Mei-Mei, things on sale are supposed to be cheaper."

"Ninety cents. *Em sei gon la*!" Mei-Mei said firmly, imitating the merchants Mother bargained with in the Chinatown market when they said, "That's the final price."

Mrs. Wong chuckled. "Good. How about selling them this Saturday, the day before Christmas Eve? That should be a busy time."

On their way home, Mei-Mei told Mother about the cookie sale and asked her to make a sign. "After the sale, we will have enough money for the bear!" Mei-Mei said, clapping her hands.

"Mama, please write,

SALE!
ALMOND COOKIES!
90¢ each!

Yummy! Yummy! Yummy!

Buy one now or you'll be sorry
for the rest of your life!

"Don't you think you are exaggerating a bit?" asked Mother. Mei-Mei thought the words were just right.

The sign reads:

**SALE!**
**ALMOND COOKIES!**
**90¢ each!**

Yummy! Yummy! Yummy!

Buy one now or you'll be sorry
for the rest of your life!

That Saturday, Mei-Mei woke up very early and hurried her mother to the restaurant. Mrs. Wong helped her tape up her sign and gave Mei-Mei a small basket for the cookies. When customers paid their bills, Mrs. Wong asked them if they wanted to buy some of Mei-Mei's cookies.

A girl about Mei-Mei's age bought Mei-Mei's eighth cookie. She tore the paper and gobbled it down. Mei-Mei swallowed hard. Quickly Mei-Mei took one of the last cookies, sliding it into her pocket. Then the picture of herself and her mother hugging that big, fuzzy bear came into her mind. Mei-Mei put the cookie back.

At just about dinnertime, a man ordered shrimp with lobster sauce to go and bought Mei-Mei's last cookie.

Mrs. Wong opened the cash register and took out a handful of one-dollar bills. "One, two . . . six . . . nine. Here you go." Mrs. Wong patted Mei-Mei's head. "You have a good head for business," she said.

Mei-Mei blushed.

Mrs. Wong continued, "The next time you work here, I'll give you money instead of almond cookies, OK?"

Mei-Mei nodded.

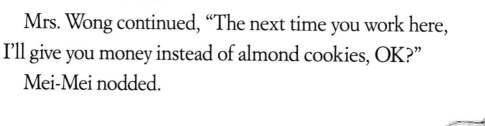

When Mei-Mei and her mother got home, Mei-Mei ran to the vase and asked Mother to watch her put in the nine dollars. It was the first time the vase had paper money inside. It looked beautiful.

"How much do we have?" Mei-Mei asked.

Mother helped her empty the vase to count the money. "Twenty-five dollars and sixty-eight cents," said Mother. "I am sorry, Mei-Mei. We don't have enough money."

Tears came to Mei-Mei's eyes. "Tomorrow is already Christmas Eve, and we can't buy the bear. How long do we have to wait for the softest, warmest bear in the whole world?"

Mother sat on the sofa and pulled Mei-Mei onto her lap. She tickled Mei-Mei until her tears stopped and Mei-Mei began to giggle. Mother put her arms around Mei-Mei and squeezed her gently. They were quiet for a while. Then Mother asked, "Am I soft?"

"Yes," said Mei-Mei.

"Am I warm?" asked Mother, smiling.

"Yes," said Mei-Mei. She suddenly understood what her mother meant.

She kissed Mother's nose and laughed. "Hey, you are my mama bear!"